MONSTERS IN THE FOG

Ali Bahrampour

Abrams Books for Young Readers

New York

For Lucia

The illustrations for this book were made with pen and ink and watercolor.

Cataloging-in-Publication Data has been applied for and
may be obtained from the Library of Congress.

ISBN 978-1-4197-5245-2

Text and illustrations © 2022 Ali Bahrampour
Book design by Heather Kelly

Printed and bound in China
10 9 8 7 6 5 4 3 2 1

Abrams Books for Young Readers are available at special discounts when purchased in
quantity for premiums and promotions as well as fundraising or educational use. Special editions can also
be created to specification. For details, contact specialsales@abramsbooks.com or the address below.

Abrams® is a registered trademark of Harry N. Abrams, Inc.

ABRAMS The Art of Books
195 Broadway, New York, NY 10007
abramsbooks.com

It's hard to knit a sweater with your hooves,
but Hakim somehow did it.
It was a present for his friend Daisy,
who lived on top of the mountain.

He packed the sweater in his saddlebag.

"She'll love it," he thought. "It gets cold up there."

It was a foggy morning.

Hakim could barely see the end of his nose.

"Where are you headed?" asked an old goat
who appeared out of nowhere.

"Up the mountain," Hakim said.

"Don't do it!" cried the goat. "There are monsters up there!"

"There are no monsters," Hakim said.

"Beware!" yelled the goat. "Beware! Beware!"

"Have a good day," said Hakim.

"You're doomed!" the old goat bleated.

Hakim had never seen a fog this thick.

"I can't let it stop me," he said.

And on he trotted.

Then he heard an awful groan. It was getting closer and closer.
Maybe that old goat was right.

Out of the mist came the strangest creature Hakim had ever seen.

But as he got closer, he saw it was only a dog carrying a board and a pile of bricks on her head.

"Help," groaned the dog. "I can't go on."

"Where are you headed?" Hakim asked.

"Over the mountain to fix up my house," said the dog.

"Put the bricks in my bag," said Hakim. "I'll bring them to the top, and then it'll be easy for you to carry them down."

"Much obliged," said the dog.

The higher they climbed, the thicker the fog got.

"What's that?" yelped the dog.

Hakim had no idea. It looked like a giant bug wiggling its many arms.

But as they got closer,
they saw a pig with
umbrellas in his backpack.

"Help!" said the pig. "I'm lost in the fog. I need to bring these umbrellas to sell on the other side of the mountain."

"We're headed the same way," said Hakim. "Come with us."

"I can't see a thing," said the pig.

"What's that up there?" asked the dog.

Hakim couldn't speak. A giant screaming skull
was heading right toward them.

But it was only a bear on a runaway tricycle.

"I can't stop!" the bear yelled.

A rock helped her out.

"I need to get my brakes fixed," said the bear.
"I'm going over the mountain to the tricycle repair shop."

Hakim told the bear to put her tricycle in the saddlebag and join them.

The climb became so tricky that the animals asked
Hakim if they could ride on his back.

"I'm scared," said the pig.

"We're doomed," said the dog.

"What if there are monsters?" asked the bear.

"Don't worry," said Hakim.

"Everything looks like a monster in the fog."

Suddenly they heard a loud scream and saw what looked like a—

"That's not a monster," said Hakim. "That's my friend Daisy!"

"Hakim!" said Daisy. "Is that you?"

"That's your friend?" asked the dog.

"Yes," said Hakim. "This is Daisy."

"But why were you screaming?" the pig asked Daisy.

"You all looked like a monster in the fog," Daisy explained. "I got scared."

"Everything looks like a monster in the fog," said Hakim.
"But the closer you get, the less scary it becomes."

The sun came out and burned away the fog.

The dog and the pig and the bear said goodbye
and headed down the mountain.

Daisy loved her sweater.

It was a perfect fit.